FAGIN

Anil PATHAK

Published by New Generation Publishing in 2020

First Edition

ISBN 978-1-80031-464-1

www.newgeneration-publishing.com

New Generation Publishing

ABOUT THE AUTHOR

Anil Pathak is a graduate, with a (Honours) Degree in Civil Engineering from the University of East London, in 1993.

Previously he has been published twice, once in December 2016 with his work The Sensuous Truth and secondly with An Indian Affair, published in 2017

His latest offering, FAGIN, although a work of fiction commemorates the works of Charles Dickens. whose literature has been a guiding light in the production of this novel.

He Describes himself as a creator and master of his own destiny. He is a keen Poet and Artist. He resides in Brighton, England, which is a constant inspiration to him, when creating his work

CONTENTS

Chapter 1: Joseph Solomon Fagin

As a boy Joseph Solomon Fagin grew up in an atmosphere of disruption and chaos. His parents left him around his time of birth. A very anxious and depressed boy, as he was. No relatives or brothers and sisters.

He always did express the opinion that he would have loved to have known his parents and have a brother, an elder brother at least. As a result of all of this his upbringing was unstable and he felt very insecure growing up.

The orphanage that he was in was in the far east of Prague, it was an antiquated looking huge building overlooking a river and a lot of greenery a nicely placed institute, fenced and the nature was beautiful.

A lonely child apart from his dear friend Toby whom he had known since he was four years of age along with Constance who would remain a lifelong friend.

All three would go out together through their early years (they had one or two years between them) they would go conker picking along the foresty country road and also blueberry picking within the forest itself, Toby knew the forest so they would never get lost.

Toby was like Fagin, in that he was insecure and blameless introverted just like Constance, but all three seemed to get on fine

Constance can be described as petite and caring and never liked her parents she was blonde and had clear blue eyes she had a memory of constantly been picked on by her parents, it could be described as a loveless relationship between both her parents and herself, as a result she looked at the world with cold eyes with a character which was strangely positive and cheerful not filled with pessimism as some would believe.

Constance loved architecture and she would stare at the building in which they lived in for ages, noticing all the crevasses and turns in the building architecture. She would go for walks on her own as she became quite tired of her bedroom surroundings. and the colours of the walls a buttermilk colour which she longed to change just as she longed to change herself. It was clear too her that she was not a normal girl.

She loved to hang with Toby and Fagin. Mostly they would seek out the grounds and not say very much to one another because they all felt that everything that needed to be said was already voiced amongst themselves.

Their rooms in the orphanage were quite far apart and it seemed like this was a comparable to their disassociation with normal kids and people. but having said that, they would form a vacuum type communication between the three of them. when in surrounding of kids and people or not. Somehow communicating with the looks on their faces the way they looked at each other. A kind of bond which was struck also between themselves thoughtful glances or woody expressions filled their faces at times. It was quite funny at times because when they were together and not in the company of people & kids, they would never talk about this weird communication that they had. You could say that in many ways these three kids were kind of special. with regards to their strangeness of their interactions. Sometimes there was no real need for words sometimes being together was all they needed to be

Toby, Fagin and Constance were engaged with a kind of perception that wasn't destructive but was like a complexity of righteous believing, with them minding their surroundings, which fascinated them from an early age.

As they grew ... through education and the lessons that life had to teach them.

They realised a deep empathy between themselves Although they were not always together, they were together Individually, they did well within the bounds that criminal education could offer them. But they shared a sadness of not really bonding with the people's, in each of their surroundings They as people, (grown adults), would not challenge this as they didn't want to

Chapter 2: The Orphanage

Joseph Solomon Fagin started life in the impoverished slums of Prague. Firstly at an orphanage, as his Parents didn't want to know him. His father regularly frequented the opium dens of Prague where he would spend many days and nights away from his unfortunate son and his prostitute, lady of the night, wife. His wife would visit the streets of Prague seeking business amongst the dark and murky alleys of the impoverished and the criminal underworld.

As a result, Joseph Fagin was a distressed and complex character. Described by his father and mother as a mistake at his birth. With no brothers or sisters to call his own, Joseph Fagin was indeed a lonesome and solitary boy with no real friends and whose daily existence was a meaningless one. There was no fortune left to him by his parents in terms of education, and learning.

Joseph Fagin would wander the markets by day stealing his daily bread and seeking along the dirty miserable streets solace and some form of happiness from his friends Toby & Constance. This daily living would continue until his 15th birthday. As an unrepentant thief he becomes involved in the bounds of a loan shark which after borrowing money for his infamous father's opium habit had become bound by this loan shark together with a few more.

Joseph Fagin had always felt wronged when his parents almost abandoned him, But he never abandoned them. He would wait at home, a shabby 1 bedroomed apartment overlooking the greater Northern divide of the City of Prague.

He found himself beside himself with worry over his parent's way of life.

He made things like a bear and a dog which he was working on, out of wood. Joseph Fagin was indeed a very good artist carving small blocks of wood with great accuracy with true resemblances, as a result, of animals such as a dog, a bear and a cow.

At 25 he could remember him thinking to himself that if he could live his life again, he wouldn't.

Debts were mounting and he (Joseph Fagin) was in constant hiding and in torment over what he should do to escape these loan sharks and debtor's prison. He decided to flee Prague and go to London where he had a few criminal acquaintances, along with Toby and Constance

The year was 1787 (27 years old, born 1760 November) August when he would eventually leave Prague for a new life in the slums of London. with little money, he would work as a street artist and magician to make ends meet. He met with his criminal friends Toby & Constance who persuaded him to accept stolen goods and sell them on.

On several occasions Fagin's mind frequented the din of several brothels which he became well known for, as a fence. He would take opiates smoking opium and Hashish to combat his ongoing state of depression.

As an artist he never amounted to much. His artwork was described as morbid and melancholy. Pictures of dark and murky bridges with a dismal skyline. In 1797, over a duration of time, Fagin found himself at 37 years old in a jail cell where he would pass five years, for receiving and selling on stolen goods. The time spent was lonely and much time was spent in isolation, for trying to escape several times and obviously failing on three occasions. Chained to the wall of his cell, Fagin's mind was suffering profoundly, his depression became worse with no opiates to help him

He threatened the Governor of the prison, saying "One day I shall kill you". Further terms of isolation beckoned for Fagin and having been chained to the wall with shackles on his feet and hands he cried to himself rambling at the same time to himself. He was in a very sorry state.

With almost no good times to reminisce on he would often think on his time growing up in the realms of the orphanage with his friends Toby and Constance who would join him in London, England and they all flee together around the right time.

All three had an incredible ethos that crime can pay, depending on how hard you would work on it! An ethos, which in all its splendour wasn't helping Fagin much, at present. Oh, how he longed for the comfort of an opium pipe at present. How he remembered from the past, how it helped him in his torn moments of anguish and depressed states of mind. As was what was one that he was facing now.

He finally was in a mood about thinking of his first time love, ... Constance whom he loved from the first time that he saw her and with each day/month that past with them being together first with Toby and Constance obviously being like A pack of three and then just with Constance: so the time they spent together equated to falling in love with her from Fagin's viewpoint, but sadly Constance had a different gaze on the relationship, the love was not requited (she was quite confused) and as Fagin (through the months) had felt this from her. His depression really was apparent in his mind, but he didn't act on it. His nightmare was caused (his depression that is) by the non-feeling from Constance who he proclaimed to his self as his first love.

For Fagin it all started when Fagin was in his manner quite a moral young man. But his feelings for Constance would send him and his emotions the other way, to being immoral. This was Fagin's problem with his love for the girl he couldn't get her out of his head although on the other hand Constance didn't think of him as nearly enough as he thought about her, Constance was in love with Fagin. And they would both elope or flee to the slums of London.

Fagin remembered, when he took her to see his mother who was never really impressed with Fagin as he didn't show any attributes to anything which was good. He did try working in the outdoor market with a friend of his mother's whilst at the tender age of nineteen, but Fagin would not be so honest about giving the money that he had earned, when it was time, at the end of the day to relinquish what he had earned from the market stall because the friend, Vladislav, would leave him on his own. Fagin would never be honest, where money was concerned, which would often get him into trouble.

When Fagin's mother would meet Constance, his mother shared with her, her bitter disappointment in Fagin as he would be given chance after chance of trying to make his life good and really productive in a positive way. But I suppose she thought... like father, like son and admittedly it all came to be truthful. Fagin, she explained, would always have a problem with authority, a lifelong aversion to it. He could never be at ease with the authorities. It's as if he had corruption in his brain, in his mind, especially, when it came to the police.

Chapter 3: Nuremberg

Fagin would leave Prague making for the East India docks of London, England. The journey would be long and arduous. His real life collision with himself and his problems with life never stopped.

On leaving Prague he made his way to Nuremberg crossing over to Germany where he would visit the Palace de Justice and the ruins of the Zeppelin fields contemplating whilst smoking on some opium with his pipe. Contemplating on time and what it has in store for him. while crossing into Nuremburg he met a recent acquaintance in the shape of a cabin boy on the wreck of a large barge whose captain was the only one out of three vessels that would give him passage for nothing.

The boy called Luca, in conversation, revealed the whereabouts of a small criminal gang operating in the heart of the city who were mainly concerned with selling and receiving stolen goods.

Fagin would spend some time in this port getting to know the criminal underworld more closely. There were many estates in Nuremburg with wealthy residents occupying plush housing estates where the thieves would concentrate their efforts and do well in salvaging stolen artefacts from such properties

Fagin's expertise lied in as a fence where he would receive stolen goods and sell them on to wealthy merchants, coming in & out of Nuremburg all the time always on the lookout for exquisite artefacts of any kind. Fagin would supply the goods and buy or exchange goods all the time whilst dodging the loan sharks who were hot on his tail from Prague, who he owed quite a lot of money too

Fagin would always be true to his belief of no love of god but in Fagin, "Yes, I am Fagin" he said "Fagin the man who loves his kind and his associates. Fagin who would believe in his own and his kind." Yes, I am Fagin and then he would meet on those those of his kind and his associates he would try to make them as he was. He would try!!

His manner was that of a supercilious & nefarious nature. Ultimately this was Fagin in a couple of words always taking on the Police in his own way alongside the parochial authorities. His superciliousness was a direct result of his aversion to the authorities. He made his bread on this character. And he never knelt down to them to whom he called the Plague. Remembering his frequent visits to the Palace de Justice at Nuremburg and remembering what he felt about those who allowed the dictatorship of the authorities, to fall on them to absorb them and to love them, Fagin turned his head in disgust and shamed upon them, the word fallacy.

Around noon he would meet with Luca and his gang. He would invest time in the gang members who he came to adore, for, they did so much for him. They made him feel whole. As his hatred for the authorities was apparent more than apparent, he would never be superficial

He would always automatically turn his energies when alone too despondency leading to his love or what came to be his love of opium and his beloved pipe. The true nature of Fagin was hard to fathom it was like his self was a split personality consumed of self-loathing. He would always contain his emotions because when he was dejected he was stoned and he was fed up of thinking because he couldn't maintain his thoughts as they would be too much effort (it seemed) to maintain them It was as though he didn't give a damn, in his lonely tune, that is, when he was playing it, quite frequently alone.

Fagin's mind was like a compass, where he knew his destiny would be as far away from the place he had left behind, (Prague), to the underworld of the East End of London. But he knew that he would travel to several ports along the way his route was all planned out. He would consolidate on his new acquaintances in Nuremburg and take to the sea again visiting in turn Bamberg then too Wurzburg both being prominent cities in their own right where he would stay at least as long as possible to know or figure out the lay of the land and then to ultimately confuse the predators, (the loan sharks) who were pursuing him throughout Prague not knowing that Fagin had fled Prague, for Germany, in the first instance. Or at least that was Fagin's thoughts.

The loan sharks, were confused as to how he (Fagin) had found the means to flee Germany as soon as they had heard or found out that indeed he had fled Prague by questioning his father, who reluctantly told them that of Fagin's whereabouts in Germany or at least the area as his father too didn't know exactly where Fagin was. Vladislav, one of the loan sharks had left Fagin's father for dead as he and his associates (Vladislav's associates), could not afford to leave Fagin's father alive, as he was a loose end. And Vladislav couldn't have that, so they gave him an overdose of opium forcing him to smoke it in front of them choking violently, literally to his death. They then left him in the ransack accommodation that he dwelled upon in pursuit of Fagin with their new information, that Toby and Constance were also somewhere in Germany. Neither could he have Fagin's mother left alive as she was always in and around the criminal underworld of the slums of Prague, she would be harder to pin down. He (Vladislava) would decide to deal with her later leaving his associates, Drav and Lusius to try to infiltrate the criminal underworld in pursuit of Dracma (Fagin's mother). Vladislav had little to go on but as he knew he was not seen around Fagin’s fathers hovel; he was free of suspicion from the law. He was thus, free to pursue Fagin more comprehensively, which he did, in time.

Chapter 4: Vladislav

Leaving the port of Nuremburg Fagin had no idea of what was happening in Prague with his father or mother but he had his suspicions that Vladislav and his associates wouldn't leave them alone and so he thought very quickly that he was not safe in Germany for long so it was time to move on.

Shortly after Vladislav had left Prague Toby and Constance were joined with Fagin at Nuremburg port. They had news of Fagin's father and they would share what they knew with Fagin to Fagin's dismay and disgust.

Fagin along with shortly Toby and Constance would leave Nuremburg for Bamburg and then quickly onto Wurzburg.

Fagin vowed that he would avenge his father's death to himself. He visited Luca and his associates before he left Nuremberg telling him that once he reached England he would send for Luca and that he in turn would set up shop within the East End of London with his contacts in and around the outskirts of Bow and Bethnal Green in the East End slums of London.

Fagin knew that he was living on borrowed time with Vladislav in hot pursuit Fagin also knew that he couldn't kill Vladislav with the help of an assassin as he couldn't pay anybody with anything as he didn't have the immediate funds needed for such a luxury. But he desperately knew that he had to dispose of Vladislav and quickly as he would prove a hinderance to Fagin's plans. What Fagin had learnt from his friends Toby and Constance was that his father died sadly at the hands of Vladislav and that his mother Dracma's whose life was also in jeopardy. He feared for his mother's life but couldn't do anything to help her at the moment.

All three quickly left for Bamburg with the help of a sympathetic captain of a cotton vessel who would promise Fagin a free passage to Bamburg.

Fagin was in a low mood lower than normal and no friend or friends could console him over his father's death.

Although Fagin at birth was called a mistake by both his parents and abandoned to an orphanage. He had an incurable love for his parents because they were simply his parents. And that, to Fagin's mind was a priceless luxury which for some reason he was proud off. Simply the fact that he had parents and that in an orphanage there were masses that did not. He remembered helping his father with supplying him with money for his opium habit, Fagin was proud of that fact too! Although Dracma, (his mother) had very little to do with Fagin from an early age, she, after marrying his father had very little to do with him too! She quickly delved into a life of drink and prostitution, excessive prostitution. A victim of debauchery, Dracma had started life in an orphanage also. Never knowing her real parents who in turn abandoned her at the tender age of two years old with only her name to show for the relationship she had with her parents, she was a bitter woman, never really understanding why she was abandoned apart from drawing the obvious conclusion that she just wasn't wanted by them.

She learnt that in her teens her father had committed suicide and her mother was never heard off. And the fact that Dracma had no knowledge of her, pleased her. But really Dracma had always felt alone with no kindred spirit to really call her own, from the orphanage, or her marriage which she only agreed to, due to her pregnancy which was a complete blow to her as it happened. Although Petr had insisted that they should get married and give the child a name was the only real reason for marriage. The marriage which fell apart from the word 'go'. This was the reason (as it was a loveless marriage) that Fagin was abandoned. But Fagin's father did have some feeling towards Fagin. A name that he had chosen for him. Dracma made it clear that she had no thought or care for Fagin or indeed for Petr, (the father).

Fagin knew that Dracma had no love for him or his father, hence the way she lived her life as a so called lady of the night was an obvious choice for her. Fagin knew very little about his mother's background, but he did feel real affection for her. And to think that she could be pursued by loan sharks and possibly killed was not something that Fagin could face.

Fagin consulted with Toby who was in fact quite a burly looking man who could easily defend himself as he was well known in some vicinities of Prague as a bar brawler, plus a drunkard being somewhat reckless in his manner, but very protective of Fagin as he knew what Fagin knew about (Fagin's past life) growing up in an orphanage with him and Constance.

He talked at length with Toby about possibly going back to Prague and dealing with the crisis with regards to Dracma in relation to her safety. But Fagin knew that Dracma had many friends in the criminal fraternity and that she was clever, she didn't really lose her head apart from particular spells of her drinking which she did frequently, drinking that is but not really losing her head unless she had cause too.

They decided upon a course of action which would secure the safety of Dracma or so they thought and to message an aid in Prague who was known to Toby and was loyal and honest to Toby And so could be trusted to look after Dracma's interests without her knowing. This was Toby's promise to Fagin. Fagin was content at that.

Chapter 5: A Duty to Morality

Fagin indeed was a fiend for any amount of money. It could be said that Fagin was the epitome of taste and elegance. All that money had to offer. And he wished the same for the people that he loved and had always loved. Constance was such a person, he doted on her, and his love was requited. Their love had to be kept abay for some time as they had no time to make a rash of things in that they were not able to finalise on their love for all the circumstances and further situations that they found themselves in, particularly Fagin.

Fagin had fallen for Constance the moment he had met her at the orphanage all those years ago, as a boy. At the time Constance was not as heartfelt as Fagin was. It could be said that she was quite confused about the whole idea of love. And her wishes, were to be rid of the orphanage as soon as was possible and to be loved by elders who would know her, in turn Although she was an intelligent child she did grow to be positive and caring with not much love or mind for pessimism as some would believe.

As far as Fagin was concerned Constance fell in love with him in her teens when they were very much together, she could remember having fond memories of conker picking in the forest which surrounded the orphanage although Constance wasn't as vocal as Fagin would have liked. She made her strong feelings of love and affection clear to Fagin at an early age (around seventeen years old).

Constance would act as a runner for Fagin. Running from place to place bringing and basically transporting stolen goods to and from the buyers and sellers and to Fagin, she loved the work and she would work alongside Toby (another dear friend of Fagin's), to make this work possible.

Depending on where they were, they along with Fagin would figure out the lay of the land. They would get to know their soon to be new acquaintances which were in the form of pawnbrokers and child pickpockets and certain coves (men) who would rob the high end establishments bringing their objects and artefacts to Toby and Constance who would either visit them or would meet at a designated place.

Fagin (as was understood by Toby and Constance), would resign himself to the local opium dens as he was troubled by his father's death and what possible outcome Toby's friend had to do with his mothers, (Dracma's) safety along with his own misery where life was concerned.

Although he was very close to Constance he wouldn't (apart from the obvious, regarding his father's death and his mother) admit to Constance or Toby, what it was, that was troubling him.

During Fagin's time of smoking opium and taking laudanum (which was an opiate, this was something he took infrequently) he would delve into pure fiction, in that, what would life would be like if his parents were normal, for example, that they were prosperous in their chosen fields of work Good works helping the disadvantaged and the paupers and orphans which littered the streets of Prague. And that they were happy and content in what they were achieving with the impoverished And how that would have a positive effect on him, (Fagin), with regards to his life and dreams and his choice of work, which he dreamt that he would follow in his parents footsteps and prove to be as successful as they were, And in turn, the blossoming feelings of love and adoration that he felt for Constance. And his ring of friends who would be joyous with Fagin knowing what Fagin had achieved and what he was about to achieve (with his parents help).

But no, ... no there was no help for the way he was full of derision and contemptment for his fellow man who poisoned him morally and in an inhumane way.

Fagin would always return (in his dream's) to what was. And how he had turned out. He resented himself and that horrid truth of what he had become. Inside he was seething and so angry, of himself. Of him not having a steady and prosperous life, which he saw in Prague wealthy Socialites, young socialites and their respective societies.

How he was forced to live in squalor and how dismissive he was of it, and that fact that his parents, (although he held love firm for them) never helped him but did the opposite and called him a mistake from the day he was born... cut Fagin's soul in two. Polluting it with feelings of rage and anger that one couldn't possibly comprehend. and why he should actually hate them for the way that they left him. But he didn't.... and why was that so?... he had no answers for it. And the fact that there were only three people he could count on in his miserable world, himself included, the others being, Toby and Constance

How he hated life and the people in it. for making him feel dejected and refused by society. How lonesome he felt, this being the reason for him not making an honest woman out of Constance, which he truly wanted to do. And how truly, he wanted revenge against his parents for putting him down and in an orphanage which he detested in the strongest possible way Fagin would always relay to himself his feelings and self-loathing and loathing. For himself and for his parents, respectively, and for life and those that got without working a day in their lives, for what they had.

Then he remembered something that was thrust upon him as a child by one of the workers in the orphanage.... "Fair... Fair... only a fool believes in fairness my friend... He also remembered someone saying to him that "the grieving moment is often the truest of moments. Full of pain and disarray as it might be, there comes from it, a glimmer, of hope, who knows where this hope comes from, but it does!!"

But these words spoken didn't convince Fagin that in a hopeless circumstance and fate there was no hope in those depressed situations.

No wonder Fagin grew up to be a villain, a Charlatan, a waster, and loafer. No wonder he couldn't commit to his feelings for Constance or too humanity as a whole. Fagin's low spirits from loss of hope or feeling of dejection created despondency in his soul character which in turn gave him no confidence in his surroundings. All this ultimately would lead to his love of money!! Wealth, taste, and elegance these things gave Fagin his confidence in himself. And his opium addiction would give him something to look forward too and a new misguided morality which he would swear by, lasting on through to his latter years.

One thing that Fagin did have was to bounce back after taking opium because his dreams and the delving of them would almost assuredly be the same. And so, although his thoughts were dangerous thoughts to have, he would most certainly contain them for his own quiet moments of grieving, which he never really grew out of.

But for business he had to keep a clear head, for Constance he had to do the same

Chapter 6: Rudesheim

And so, onto Rudesheim and Cocham. Fagin had a love for Rudesheimer Schloss perched by the river, where he would take Constance and the Rheingau in the Rhine Valley along with the beautiful Mediterranean style setting of vineyards and valleys and surrounding forest. Showing also the history of winemaking at the Rheingau Wine Museum, set in Bromserberg Castle an 11th Century architectural wonder.

Also, Fagin showed her the Siegfried's Mechanical Music Museum set in a 16th Century noble court which displays a fine selection of automated instruments which were all new in the 18th Century.

At the foot of the Taunus Mountains and overlooking the Rhine stands the picturesque town of Rudesheim surrounded by sweeping valleys and lush green valley's where in the mountains Fagin and Constance would have signs of Falcon's eagles and the exquisite surrounding countryside.

They walked along the Drosselgasse, a delightful cobbled street lined by old timbered houses that crawls with vines, was where Rhine boatmen found food and lodging in the 15th Century where this enchanting place was filled with boutiques and old fashioned Taverns.

This was where Fagin would seek out more recent acquaintances of his trade, of receiving and selling stolen goods...

Toby had heard from his friend in Prague. According to him, Dracma had been arrested for soliciting, she had been imprisoned for 18 months as this was not the first time she had dealings with the law over soliciting in the suburbs of Prague.

This news was somewhat a kind of relief for Fagin, but she could still be got at in prison by Vladislav's associates and the friends that they might have in prison.

Vladislav himself had returned to Prague now that the heat was off him for potentially being put in the frame for Petr's murder. In which case Petr's departure from their world had been put down to misadventure and possible suicide. The Courts were satisfied and so this meant that Vladislav was apparently in the clear. He was therefore free to continue his business that he had as a successful pawnbroker/loan shark in the provinces. He had left it to his associates to follow Fagin to the end if needs be to get back the money that Fagin had mindfully borrowed.

Fagin knew that what he had borrowed could never amount to much in Vladislav's eyes. For the kind of money that Vladislav was used to handling was much more than Fagin had borrowed. But Vladislav was a greedy and not human thinking man, when it came to the people that he had borrowed money too. He was purely demonic. As this character trait was one that had built his more than successful business in the provinces of Prague.

But Fagin didn't know that Vladislav's partner, well two of them, had found the Captain that had helped Fagin to cross into Nuremburg and further on.

They had put him to the same ordeal as they did with Petr, (Fagin's father). They questioned the Captain Lazurus and with a lot of persuasion and a few strong pipes of opium which Lazurus was forced to take. They found out that Fagin had reached the port of Rudesheim and was bound for Luxembourg in the coming weeks, via Cocham, (the village off).

Jan (one of Vladislav's associates/Partners) had hung Lazurus on his own vessel. Burnt the vessel around him leaving it in the Port of Nuremburg, to which Lazurus had returned for a brief period. But he was never to leave, he was hung for a definite period of time before Jan removed the supports to his feet, making sure that he would see his vessel torched before he died, totally overwhelmed by the laudanum and opium that Jan and his friend cruelly administered. Lazurus was in a state of madness (just before he died). As he had never dabbled in drugs in his lifetime Jan left the body to burn with the vessel and set out for Rudesheim.

Chapter 7: The Opium Den

The Opium Den was exquisite with Red walls and places to bunk, in a large arena full of pillars, a high ceiling decorated with a fancy and flamboyant kind of shape of a pair of dragon's enjoying a duel with another, the walls were also decorated with silver and Red and Fagin felt at home here.

It was on the outskirts of a town called Cocham, on a derelict site, underground, beneath a torn down tavern, standing on its own. Fagin looked around and recognised the ones who were just lying there with far away looks in their eyes a look he had met many times before. But he never seen the like of the name. The Tavern on the way Opium Den which was what it was called by the people who knew the place. With Silk sheets and large round pillows, pillows of all shapes and sizes draped alongside the picturesque floor and surrounding artwork and artefacts. Yes, it was a glamorous setting and cosy pictures of the Rhine River (overlooking it). And the proud large estates of wealth, and stature was a beautiful arrangement, thought Fagin.

Constance knew where he was and disliked it very much but at the same time, she would understand why he frequented such places. Their almost cavalier decadence the showing of extravagance and the words which spelt "The smoke never lies" on one of the walls, in silver, made Constance feel almost sick with such a strong smell of opium normally smoked in pipes, just occupying the air of the opium den. Overwhelming in its arrival into the arena, of people. The room as Fagin noticed was always half full of wasters who would smoke for pleasure, smoke because of some grievance they had with themselves or of people or of life: people from all walks of life would gather here and that's what Fagin liked. The momentous generation as Fagin would put it "are striving forward meeting adversity as it rears its ugly head, going forward and taking it on in their own capacities, lying down enjoying the dancing doped up girls of which there were 8 or 9 just dancing to sitar music. One would only need to stand for a while and soon that person, would be affected by the essence of the smoke and thus, have to sit or lay down.

Fagin would wander around the arena and soak in the beautifully laden tapestry on the ceiling and the enormous arrangement of art and artefacts that were just standing there. He would roam around for 25 minutes until he had to sit or lay down and buy some for his favourite pipe which he always carried with him.

Sinking his head on one of the raised cushions he would be met by a dancing girl who would be lighting Fagin's pipe. Then she would dance for him sexfully, Fagin's eyelids would drop to half-mast and he would look at her affectionately, reminding him of Constance, as she was the only constant thing in his life. He knew he always had the choice of talking with her about his hang-ups or to smoke the pipe, but he always chose the pipe. He somehow felt at one with his pipe a beautifully carved device about seven inches long and an extraordinary motif engraving of a Serpent on the side of the barrel.

Beginning his dream again as he closed his eyes. But he first thought about the arduous journey two nights before on a fishing vessel after hearing from Toby that Captain Lazurus had been silenced by Vladislav.

He would have to think up a plan to deal with Jan and his friend Vladislav after all.

He would set out Toby's friend to the criminal underworld of Cocham and say to a few that Fagin would be at the Rhine Tavern at a supposed time, where he would be on his own, completely vulnerable then Fagin's friends would surround the tavern and seek out Jan and Sasha, (Vladislav's partners), and do to them, what they had done to Fagin's dear father and to a good friend in the captain.

Fagin knew that they were on their way from Rudesheim to Cocham, and apparently travelling very fast. They would be there in a few days, in Cocham.

Fagin had it all planned. First a beating by some of Fagin's more muscular friends. Then enough opium to draw them to madness and then he would hang them from the tavern beams. High up there.

Within two and three quarters of a day this is what happened. To Fagin's delight.

Fagin would take his revenge when the tide flowed in his favour on the two who murdered the two people that he was close too in Fagin's mind. And the rest ... well Fagin was not going to let anyone compromise his lasting friends and love, in any way. He would torch the bodies to eradicate any such evidence of Jan and Sasha.

But there was still Vladislav, and the two who were after his mother. Fagin would have to think on some more. Drav and Lusius the two who were still in Prague would be sent, Fagin was sure. But surely it would take Vladislav at least a week to find out what had happened to Jan and Sasha, & to know that Fagin had strong suspicions that Vladislav was on to Fagin.

Chapter 8: The Fleeing of Cocham

The fishing vessel of Captain Versales was soon to dock Fagin and Constance. Toby would sail later on; Fagin and the Captain would partake in much wine and the playing of cards while they waited on arrival to Luxembourg Constance was resting.

Captain Versales was something of a Poet and Fagin was very interested in hearing a few. This is how they go:-

By The River.

I tripped over a wire today.
I just didn't see it as it was.
Camouflaged with Hay
Some hours before, I heard such a wonderful song
from a robin that sat all day long
as I lay beside the smell of the barn
I could feel the warmth of the wind
as it crept past.
The Colours in the sky played on my eye
as I reached for the shade that was sitting close by
As I lay there wrestling with the concrete floor
there inside me was a pain I couldn't ignore
As I pondered on that day after a month
or more, sitting in the park I heard the same
song as it was sung before
The song was there in my mind for sure
I smiled and glanced over the river and did
think, no more.

A Far Cry

Real is the vision
truth in the reason
warmth is the feeling
In yourself you must believe in
For in your eyes, shows me a feeling of no demise
I can feel that you are so wise
One learns a lesson on the answer to a question
One learns the question according to one's perception
as one thinks thoughts that may astound him
it may prove to be too profound for our understanding
the way we steer the paddles of our mind.
may show one, the things that he had left behind, or aside
Truth in reason
Surely must show us the day, as we ask for guidance
from the lord, as we prey.

Find It.

Love is the force that will bind us
trouble may one day find us
It may become a test, that will challenge us.
But we will prosper in the time that God gave us.
I do not know what life has in store
but I know now that love is something that one does
not have to endure
So, love in the first and love in the last
that's the way to beat the demons at last.

A Tale.

A lion never lies,
it tricks you with disguise
slowly walking along its way
as it hopes to see its prey
The eagle has its eyes,
Seeking as it travels through the skies
Watching close by a tiger, as it swats a fly
All these creatures so menacing
as they try to figure out the world they're in
They really have no time
to contemplate piece of mind
They really have to go
to get on, to get on, with the show

Fagin shrugged at when the last part of "A Far Cry" was read. He had no belief in God, so he didn't think that we "asked for guidance as we "prey".

"Guidance is found from within," Fagin explained.

"Guidance is a hope that we all cling too."

"Guidance in providence is a long tale of fallacy," explained Fagin.

What your heart feels the mind will obey too what the eyes see, the soul will laugh or cry too. Would you listen to some of mine, Fagin said, the Captain said. "I would welcome it, Fagin!"

Emotion – unlock the mystery

Crying only shows the remorse that you feel.
lying only shows the hate that you conceal
If one succumbs to what is vile
So much, so that it leaves a cruel smile
Then within you something will grow
and it will hide from you what you should know
Until you crave for the knowledge hidden

from so long, so long ago
And now you are so old, and your energy has
left you for cold
and nothing replaces it, but the hate when you first felt it
Don't you wish that you cried instead?
So that you might have laid peacefully in your bed?

In You.
I heard you whisper from where it can't be told
I see you gaze at yourself when you were not too old.
I saw you smile, you seemed too pleased
with yourself as you were never ignored
The glory of the morning was so divine
as you stood facing it, as you sipped your wine
wrinkled you may be and whispering that
you now know and who's to say what magic will follow.

The Captain said that's all very well Fagin but listen to this one.

Call Him.
You know life is so scary
and life is so cold
when you've got no one to hold
I know that I'm alone
and I know the feeling of emptiness
But there is God and he will always be there
I know he'll take away the feelings of despair
I know that I'm blessed because I know him
while the four winds are a blowing
he will save us from loathing.

No matter how you deny in your no love of god. In this poem it all seems to be making sense and they are the words of truth no matter which way you look at it! so long as that way is not yours Fagin!

Fagin laughed, and thus continued to deal the cards. It was a nervous laugh as he couldn't hide the way it came about. "Yes" Fagin admitted, "There could be some truth in what you say!"

Chapter 9: The Port of No Return

According to Toby the remains of the bodies of Jan and Sasha were recovered by the Police and Fagin had just reached Luxembourg worrying that enough of the remains could be found. Enough to recognise the bodies.

The muscular companions of Fagin were careless they had left enough to be of evidential interest to the Police.

The companions of Fagin were quickly apprehended but they knew themselves to be stealthy where Fagin's involvement was concerned as they knew with Fagin, they would reap rewards later on in life. Nothing was said, by Fagin, in these delicate times of survival, for Constance and Fagin. For everything was understood by Fagin's companions of which there were three of them. They were sent on to Penal Colonies near Cocham and stayed there for the next 27 years. Being found guilty of murder having been sighted on the surrounding countryside of the old Rhine Tavern, at the Rhine there were travellers on this derelict patch who had spotted Fagin's companions. They were doomed but they did what was expected off them, an agreement they had with themselves. As a token too honour amongst thieves/criminals. Fagin promised them their Glory and to take care of Vladislav.

Toby reacted to Fagin's message to flee Cocham and join him in Riems in France where they would go on to the East India Docks in the heart of London, in about a month from now. Fagin's head was nearly about to explode.

By now Vladislav had received word that his two partners Jan and Sasha were dead. "Fagin will pay for their deaths" shrieked Vladislav. "I will get back the money that he stole from me!!

Constance tried to console Fagin but failed. Fagin was too hot-headed to be consoled.

But unluckily for Vladislav, the police had seen a connection between Jan and Sasha and himself. After questioning of Fagin's companions, one then muttered (worse for wear) that they had (Jan and Sasha) been sent by Vladislav to kill them and so the plot was to thus capture Jan and Sasha and deal with them accordingly. Vladislav was later arrested and sent to prison in Prague, where he remained for his entire life.

Fagin's companions made out that they were owed money by Vladislav and that his answer was to send Jan & Sasha instead to eradicate the debt by eradicating Fagin's companions. But they couldn't plead self-defence due to the fact that the whole thing was premeditated murder, which Fagin's companions admitted too.

But this wasn't the end of the true debt that he owed Vladislav. So, Vladislav sent more men to deal with Fagin.

Fagin would guess that it would be the case that more would come. Especially now that Vladislav had been imprisoned, for life.

And according to Toby's friend, Fagin's reasoning was confirmed.

Unfortunately, Toby's friend was found out by the criminal underworld and he was dealt with in a most horrific way, he was bludgeoned to death by those who travelled to Toby's friend, those who were sympathetic to Vladislav and his plight. Before Toby's friend died, he was questioned, and the sympathizers of Vladislav's plight found out about Toby as well.

Toby was also aware of the fact that he'd be hunted, and his position was not a safe or good one. He had to flee to London as soon as possible. To even consider himself to be safe, as he would be then with Fagin by that time.

Fagin was living with the travelling Volleurs a band of gypsies. Constance was by his side, frail of the travelling and very weary of the journey from Cocham to Luxembourg She would sleep for most of the day they arrived. Fagin would visit the infamous taverns opium den which he frequented for the next two and a half weeks. He had no time to visit the many castles or the surrounding countryside except when he travelled with the Gypsies, he'd eat hedgehog (cooked) and goulash, which was made from the technique of braising. But as Fagin had to respect his Jewish way life in the way of food to eat, he would avoid Pork and shellfish, he would only eat meat or poultry that was certified as being kosher. Which was a hard thing when travelling with the Volleurs. As their food was very much stew based with Pork and shellfish being a common ingredient.

Fagin would not feel safe until unless he arrived at the East India dock in the heart of London. And then to set up shop in Bethnal Green and Bow. And also, that he was safe with his underworld friends there.

He wrote a poem to himself in honour of the country England called Sycamore.

Sycamore

Far from belief, North from relief
lives two giant emotions, called love and devotion.
Superseded no
Counterbalance to woe?
I suppose I believe it to be so
The fields we do roam
upon decisions we do form
The Sky as it brightens again
and our minds, some may sometimes implore
because we have no belief to ignore
Oh well let's see what's in store, as we take a Seat
by the beloved Sycamore.

Luxembourg was a vast place with lots of pretty castles with pretty names.

But he had no time to align himself with prettiness as he was facing sheer ugliness in the shape of Vladislav's associates who were bound to be on Fagin's tail, as soon as he would reach London, England he would be safer and more secure. With the money he had and the consignments waiting to be sent from Nuremberg and Rudesheim he could easily set up a Pawnbroker's as a front for receiving those consignments (stolen goods), and to lay those artefacts on to rich buyers, who would be there in England in their multiples. There were rich pickings to be had in London and all neighbouring cities. Just another week before he would reach The Reims in France.

Chapter 10: Reims, France

Captain Versales already was in agreement with Fagin that they would reach Paris in a matter of weeks via Reims in France. Fagin would make time to see the Tau Palace or the Palace of Tau in Reims, France and also the Notre Dame de Reims Cathedral in Reims as they were next to each other.

And also, St Nicolas Chapel of Tau Palace, Reims France.

There were the La Vie de la Vierge (life of the Virgin) tapestries that Fagin wanted to see, he saw it as a historical place in its entirety. Reims was a centre of tapestry production in the 16th century and also a place of learning which really appealed to Fagin – Reims University founded in 1547 Bibliotheque de la Ville (library) founded in 1809. And also, the birth of Champagne. The Champagne house of Gosset was founded as a still wine producer in 1584 Ruinart was founded in 1729 and was soon followed by Chanoine Freres (1730), Taittinger (1734), Moet et Chondon (1743) and Veuve Clicquet (1772).

The vicinity of Reims was also famous for its many vineyards and its extensive forests and rolling hills.

Fagin basically had no time to visit these astounding places, the only thing Fagin had time for was opium and Constance who was travelling with him and even the time he gave her was limited.

Fagin knew that this whole arduous journey had taken its toll on the both of them, especially Constance. He especially wanted her to rest as much as she could.

He would take Constance to see the Palace of Tau in Reims and also the Notre-Dame de Reims Cathedral in Reims and also the Saint Nicholas Chapel at Tau Palace

Reims France. and also, the La vie de la Vierge (life of the virgin) tapestries. Constance was amazed and bewildered by the open show of such a palace and places.

But they couldn't forget that they were on the run from Vladislav's associates who were hot on their trail having just left Luxembourg for Reims.

Paris was hardly 6 days away from Reims – it was approximately (144 kilometres) or 90 miles by vessel, and then to Calais. So, to allow two weeks for the journey to Calais from Paris was quite considerable a journey after the laborious journey from Prague.

Fagin once again, slipped into depression as a symptom of his multiple anxieties. As he was at sea, pondering on his mental ailments/disorders. The only good thing in his life was Constance and her love for him. Fagin desperately tried to forget his troubles and removed his pipe from his person and threw it in the water.

He glanced at his ledger, the debt fell into hundreds, but his stock was considerable in places where he had left it, a substantial amount of garden dressings, artefacts and artwork was in Nuremberg with Luca and his criminal gang. They were keeping a close eye on it.

Word had it that his stock was growing in Luxembourg with the Volleurs (the Gypsies) as they were in that way themselves seeking out the proud gentry and its accommodations Fagin would receive at least fifty percent of the plunder with the deal he had struck with them.

Fagin loved to read exactly what was in the ledger. He would price each item meticulously and keep an accurate description of each piece.

Fagin and Constance were walking on the deck of the vessel, they talked of the years at the orphanage and the true friendship they had, the three of them.

And of course, the associates of Vladislav who were possibly in Reims by now.

"All we have to do is to make it to London my dear," Fagin explained, "and we will be safe they would would not dare to travel on to England in fear of the reprisals that they would have to endure ... not for six hundred guinea's," which was two thirds of the amount that he owed.

Fagin promised Constance that he would make her a lady, once they were in London, England. Although Constance showed little enthusiasm for any such title the only title, she craved for was to be the wife of Fagin.

Fagin wasn't ready for such a commitment. "Let things die down for a couple of years, my dear, then we will think about the future, my dear." But he wasn't terribly vocal about the subject. He was more interested in his business ideas and the shipment of consignments from Germany and Luxembourg to London, England and he knew that the world was his oyster. When settled, in London, he would recruit his own boys and offer them food and lodging in return for the plunder.

"In a few years I will enter society as an equal ... my dear, you know that has always been my dream, my dear." Fagin added.

They both looked out onto the waters noticing the reflection of the surrounds in the water It was so innocent, so beautiful, as beautiful as all the tapestries they had seen together and the bourgeois chateau's in France that they glimpsed and visited.

They took one look at each other, held hands and kissed with much feeling of affection and devotion they had for each other.

They left the gaze of the waters and Fagin followed Constance, below deck, they undressed each other in the cabin they had shared for nearly a fortnight and for the first time they once again lay beside each other and made love.

Chapter 11: Calais, The Arrival

They arrived in Calais in just a few days and straight away they would visit the famous hotel, The Hotel de l'Angleterre which had its own theatre and carriage hire – it was said to be the finest in Europe.

They also visited The Citadel of Calais which was a fortress constructed on the ruins of a medieval castle dating from the 13th Century and whose purpose it was to defend the City of Calais.

Fagin and Constance met up with Toby "who had just crept in the night before, into Calais his journey was a tough one, he had a meeting with Vladislav's agents and the agents were staying in a second class timbered house with the surrounding countryside on all sides visible to the Citadel of Calais. Toby was astonished that they had made it that far." Toby was messaged by Fagin to burn the hotel rooms where the two agents delved.

And as Fagin enjoying a flamboyant lifestyle for a few days, Toby quietly planned the bombing of the two rooms at least with homemade dynamite.

The dynamite was successful. It was planted on the other side of the walls of the agents dwelling not before time, at midnight, Toby was watching the two burning adjoining rooms, while the agents slept.

There were no signs of the two agents they didn't survive. They both died by receiving extensive burns and ultimately suffocation as the windows were quite highly set in the walls of the rooms.

Fagin was not happy as he wanted a different death for them as these two agents were (as rumour had it according to the Provinces of Prague's underworld) the worst of a bad bunch of killers. Fagin had so wished to drug them first whilst painfully sticking them. Yes, Fagin was really the devil in a green overcoat. His mother Dracma was still serving in a decommissioned ship which was docked in the provinces of Prague. Attempts were made to get to her, to do her mischief but failed as the prisoners were guarded well, and the only way to the rather large Vessel was by boat but there were no side ladders running up the carriage of the vessel apart from just the one. Toby thought she was quite safe. Jail was the safest place for her, although, Dracma had no idea of what was going on, she was facing adversity on a different level. She was doomed and felt doomed which lasted for the next eight and a half months.

The three friends were united once more, at long last. They gave a sigh of relief at the sight of Toby.

Fagin really needed his mother to see sense and come to London, England to start afresh with them. But she wouldn't leave Prague, she spoke little or no English which would always be a hindrance to her. After her Jail sentence she grieved more fully of her husband's death and vowed to give up her life as the lady of the night and go to work in a rather large Tavern in one of the provinces.

Fagin was happy to hear the news of his mother's early release for good behaviour little did she know that her life was under threat, two times whilst on the ship. And according to the three it was better left unsaid.

They visited the Porte de Boulogne which provides access from the South into the Citadel of Calais. They all wished to visit the Porte de Neptune which provides access from the east into the Citadel of Calais.

Before reaching England at the East India Docks, Fagin and Constance would reminisce together holding each other in an embrace but Fagin broke loose and was more disturbed by his father's demise. As he admitted to Constance, Constance, Sighed. "Go with Toby tonight, my dear and I shall wander the skies flying high with my father tonight." explained Fagin. "Go on, my dear I will be reborn in the morning," explained Fagin.

Fagin went below into one of the cabins and pulled out a brand new pipe, gold plated and engraved with the letter 'F' into the barrel of the pipe. There was a Chinese manservant on board who would serve Fagin his pipe full of refined opium. Fagin thought no more, smiled and drifted away as he had done so many times during this troublesome but extensive voyage. He thought briefly of Captain Lazurus. And then drifted away further his mind's eye was having the sight of the eagle, he could see the turrets of various chateau's, the green green grass the rolling fields and the surrounding countryside's. It was as though the sky was a blank canvas in his dream as he flew near what seemed to be the clouds. And then suddenly Westminster Abbey came into site. "Ah London, I can see London, which his mouth spoke slowly and very softly. And then finally he fell asleep with a smile on his face.

Constance looked in on Fagin and saw a smile on his face. She was happy and she said to herself, that all ends that ends well. She had one clear choice and that was to be happy for him, for her, for Toby. The fact that they were still alive. "STILL ALIVE" she cried out, she lay beside him and joined him in sleep. Thinking on the past French Revolution as a last thought, and as she was partly French it remained in her thoughts for the rest of her days.

Two or three days later they had reached the East India Dock. Fagin was very happy there standing on the deck with Constance and Toby, all around they could see their dream, the England that they all wanted to see through the eyes of London, namely the East India Docks.

"What a pleasant view my dears!! And to the Porter who was just about to take on their luggage Fagin said, "Good Evening, my dear. They call me Fagin!

www.ingramcontent.com/pod-product-compliance
Ingram Content Group UK Ltd.
Pitfield, Milton Keynes, MK11 3LW, UK
UKHW040003200726
13854UKWH00001B/20

9 781800 314641